HORRID HENRY

AND THE
BOGEY BABYSITTER

Francesca Simon spent her childhood on the beach in California, and then went to Yale and Oxford Universities to study medieval history and literature. She now lives in London with her English husband and their son. When she is not writing books she is doing theatre and restaurant reviews or chasing after her Tibetan Spaniel, Shanti.

Also by Francesca Simon

HORRID HENRY

AND THE
BOGEY BABYSITTER

Francesca Simon
Illustrated by Tony Ross

Orion
Children's Books

First published in Great Britain in 2002
by Orion Children's Books
a division of the Orion Publishing Group Ltd
Orion House
5 Upper Saint Martin's Lane
London WC2H 9EA

An Hachette Livre UK Company

17 19 20 18 16

Text © Francesca Simon 2002
Illustrations © Tony Ross 2002

ISBN 978 1 85881 826 9

The Orion Publishing Group's policy is to use papers that
are natural, renewable and recyclable products and
made from wood grown in sustainable forests. The logging
and manufacturing processes are expected to conform to
the environmental regulations of the country of origin.

A catalogue record for this book is available
from the British Library.

Printed in Great Britain by
Clays Ltd, St Ives plc

*To my old friends Caroline Elton and
Andrew Franklin, and my new ones
Miriam, Jonathan, and Michael*

CONTENTS

1

HORRID HENRY TRICKS AND TREATS

Hallowe'en! Oh happy, happy day! Every year Horrid Henry could not believe it: an entire day devoted to stuffing your face with sweets and playing horrid tricks. Best of all, you were *supposed* to stuff your face and play horrid tricks. Whoopee!

Horrid Henry was armed and ready. He had loo roll. He had water pistols. He had shaving foam. Oh my, would he be playing tricks tonight. Anyone who didn't instantly hand over a fistful of sweets would get it with the foam. And woe betide any fool who gave him an apple. Horrid Henry knew how to treat rotten grown-ups like that.

His red and black devil costume lay ready on the bed, complete with evil mask, twinkling horns, trident, and whippy tail. He'd scare everyone wearing that.

"Heh heh heh," said Horrid Henry, practising his evil laugh.

"Henry," came a little voice outside his bedroom door, "come and see my new costume."

"No," said Henry.

"Oh please, Henry," said his younger brother, Perfect Peter.

"No," said Henry. "I'm busy."

"You're just jealous because *my* costume is nicer than yours," said Peter.

"Am not."

"Are too."

Come to think of it, what *was* Peter wearing? Last year he'd copied Henry's monster costume and ruined Henry's Hallowe'en. What if he were copying

Henry's devil costume? That would be just like that horrible little copycat.

"All right, you can come in for two seconds," said Henry.

A big, pink bouncy bunny bounded into Henry's room. It had little white bunny ears. It had a little white bunny tail. It had pink polka dots everywhere else. Horrid Henry groaned. What a stupid costume. Thank goodness *he* wasn't wearing it.

"Isn't it great?" said Perfect Peter.

"No," said Henry. "It's horrible."

"You're just saying that to be mean, Henry," said Peter, bouncing up and down. "I can't wait to go trick-or-treating in it tonight."

Oh no. Horrid Henry felt as if he'd been punched in the stomach. Henry would be expected to go out trick or treating – with Peter! He, Henry, would have to walk around with a pink polka dot bunny. Everyone would see him. The shame of it! Rude Ralph would never stop teasing him. Moody Margaret would call him a bunny wunny. How could he play tricks on people with a pink polka dot bunny following him everywhere? He was ruined. His name would be a joke.

"You can't wear that," said Henry desperately.

"Yes I can," said Peter.

4

"I won't let you," said Henry.

Perfect Peter looked at Henry. "You're just jealous."

Grrr! Horrid Henry was about to tear that stupid costume off Peter when, suddenly, he had an idea.

It was painful.

It was humiliating.

But anything was better than having Peter prancing about in pink polka dots.

"Tell you what," said Henry, "just because I'm so nice I'll let you borrow my monster costume. You've always wanted to wear it."

"NO!" said Peter. "I want to be a bunny."

"But you're supposed to be scary for Hallowe'en," said Henry.

"I am scary," said Peter. "I'm going to bounce up to people and yell 'boo'."

"I can make you really scary, Peter," said Horrid Henry.

"How?" said Peter.

"Sit down and I'll show you." Henry patted his desk chair.

"What are you going to do?" said Peter suspiciously. He took a step back.

"Nothing," said Henry. "I'm just trying to help you."

Perfect Peter didn't move.

"How can I be scarier?" he said cautiously.

"I can give you a scary haircut," said Henry.

Perfect Peter clutched his curls.

"But I like my hair," he said feebly.

6

"This is Hallowe'en," said
Henry. "Do you want to
be scary or don't you?"

"Um, um, uh," said
Peter, as Henry pushed
him down in the chair and
got out the scissors.

"Not too much," squealed Peter.

"Of course not," said Horrid Henry.
"Just sit back and relax, I promise you'll
love this."

Horrid Henry twirled the scissors.

Snip! Snip! Snip! Snip! Snip!

Magnificent, thought Horrid Henry.
He gazed proudly at his work. Maybe he
should be a hairdresser when he grew up.
Yes! Henry could see it now. Customers
would queue for miles for one of
Monsieur Henri's scary snips. Shame his
genius was wasted on someone as yucky
as Peter. Still…

"You look great, Peter," said Henry. "Really scary. Atomic Bunny. Go and have a look."

Peter went over and looked in the mirror.

"AAAAAAAAAARGGGGGGG!"

"Scared yourself, did you?" said Henry. "That's great."

"AAAAAAAAAARGGGGGGG!" howled Peter.

Mum ran into the room.

"AAAAAAAAAARGGGGGGG!" howled Mum.

"AAAAAAAAAARGGGGGGG!" howled Peter.

"Henry!" screeched Mum. "What have you done! You horrid, horrid boy!"

 What was left of Peter's hair stuck up in ragged tufts all over his head. On one side was a big bald patch.

"I was just making

8

him look scary,"
protested Henry. "He
said I could."

"Henry made me!"
said Peter.

"My poor baby," said
Mum. She glared at Henry.

"No trick-or-treating for you," said
Mum. "You'll stay here."

Horrid Henry could hardly believe his
ears. This was the worst thing that had
ever happened to him.

"NO!" howled Henry. This was all
Peter's fault.

"I hate you Peter!" he screeched. Then
he attacked. He was Medusa, coiling
round her victim with her snaky hair.

"Aaaahh!" screeched Peter.

"Henry!" shouted Mum. "Go to your
room!"

★

Mum and Peter left the house to go
trick-or-treating. Henry had screamed
and sobbed and begged. He'd put on
his devil costume, just in case his tears
melted their stony hearts. But no. His
mean, horrible parents wouldn't change
their mind. Well, they'd be sorry.
They'd all be sorry.

Dad came into the sitting room. He
was holding a large shopping bag.

"Henry, I've got some work to finish so
I'm going to let you hand out treats to
any trick-or-treaters."

Horrid Henry stopped plotting his
revenge. Had Dad gone mad? Hand out

treats? What kind of
punishment was this?
Horrid Henry
fought to keep a big
smile off his face.
"Here's the
Hallowe'en stuff,

Henry," said Dad. He handed Henry the
heavy bag. "But remember," he added
sternly, "these treats are not for you:
they're to give away."

Yeah, right, thought Henry.

"OK Dad," he said as meekly as he
could. "Whatever you say."

Dad went back to the kitchen. Now
was his chance! Horrid Henry leapt on
the bag. Wow, was it full! He'd grab all
the good stuff, throw back anything
yucky with lime or peppermint, and he'd
have enough sweets to keep him going
for at least a week!

Henry yanked open the bag. A terrible
sight met his eyes. The bag was full of

11

satsumas. And apples. And walnuts in
their shells. No wonder his horrible
parents had trusted him to be in charge
of it.

Ding dong.

Slowly, Horrid Henry heaved his heavy
bones to the door. There was his empty,
useless trick-or-treat bag, sitting forlornly
by the entrance. Henry gave it a kick,
then opened the door and glared.

"Whaddya want?"
snapped Horrid Henry.

"Trick-or-treat," whis-
pered Weepy William.
He was dressed as a
pirate.

Horrid Henry held
out the bag of horrors.

"Lucky dip!" he
announced. "Close
your eyes for a big
surprise!"

12

William certainly would
be surprised at what a
rotten treat he'd be
getting.

Weepy William put
down his swag bag, closed
his eyes tight, then plunged his hand into
Henry's lucky dip. He rummaged and he
rummaged and he rummaged, hoping to
find something better than satsumas.

Horrid Henry eyed Weepy William's
bulging swag bag.

Go on Henry, urged the bag. He'll
never notice.

Horrid Henry did not wait to be asked
twice.

Dip!

Zip!

Pop!

Horrid Henry grabbed a big handful of
William's sweets and popped them inside
his empty bag.

13

Weepy William opened his eyes.

"Did you take some of my sweets?"

"No," said Henry.

William peeked inside his bag and burst into tears.

"Waaaaaaaa!" wailed William. "Henry took – "

Henry pushed him out and slammed the door.

Dad came running.

"What's wrong?"

"Nothing," said Henry. "Just William crying 'cause he's scared of pumpkins."

Phew, thought Henry. That was close. Perhaps he had been a little too greedy.

Ding dong.

It was Lazy Linda wearing a pillowcase over her head. Gorgeous Gurinder was with her, dressed as a scarecrow.

"Trick-or-treat!"

"Trick-or-treat!"

"Close your eyes for
a big surprise!" said
Henry, holding out the
lucky dip bag.

"Ooh, a lucky dip!"
squealed Linda.

Lazy Linda and Gorgeous Gurinder put
down their bags, closed their eyes, and
reached into the lucky dip.

Dip!

Zip!

Pop!

Dip!

Zip!

Pop!

Lazy Linda opened her eyes.

"You give the worst treats ever, Henry,"
said Linda, gazing at her walnut in
disgust.

"We won't be coming back *here*,"

15

sniffed Gorgeous Gurinder.

Tee hee, thought Horrid Henry.

Ding dong.

It was Beefy Bert. He was wearing a robot costume.

"Hi Bert, got any good sweets?" asked Henry.

"I dunno," said Beefy Bert.

Horrid Henry soon found out that he did. Lots and lots and lots of them. So did Moody Margaret, Sour Susan, Jolly Josh and Tidy Ted. Soon Henry's bag was stuffed with treats.

Ding dong.

Horrid Henry opened the door.

"Boo," said Atomic Bunny.

Henry's sweet bag!
Help! Mum would
see it!

"Eeeeek!"
screeched Horrid
Henry. "Help! Save
me!"

Quickly, he ran upstairs clutching his
bag and hid it safely under his bed.
Phew, that was close.

"Don't be scared, Henry, it's only me,"
called Perfect Peter.

Horrid Henry came back downstairs.

"No!" said Henry. "I'd never have
known."

"Really?" said Peter.

"Really," said Henry.

"Everyone just gave sweets this year,"
said Perfect Peter. "Yuck."

Horrid Henry held out the lucky dip.

"Ooh, a satsuma," said Peter. "Aren't I
lucky!"

"I hope you've learned your lesson, Henry," said Mum sternly.

"I certainly have," said Horrid Henry, eyeing Perfect Peter's bulging bag. "Good things come to those who wait."

2

HORRID HENRY AND THE BOGEY BABYSITTER

"No way!" shrieked Tetchy Tess, slamming down the phone.

"No way!" shrieked Crabby Chris, slamming down the phone.

"No way!" shrieked Angry Anna. "What do you think I am, crazy?"

Even Mellow Martin said he was busy.

Mum hung up the phone and groaned.

It wasn't easy finding someone to babysit more than once for Horrid Henry. When Tetchy Tess came, Henry flooded the bathroom. When Crabby Chris came he hid her homework and

"accidentally" poured red grape juice
down the front of her new white jeans.
And when Angry Anna came Henry –
no, it's too dreadful. Suffice it to say that
Anna ran screaming from the house and
Henry's parents had to come home early.

Horrid Henry hated babysitters. He
wasn't a baby. He didn't want to be sat
on. Why should he be nice to some ugly,
stuck-up, bossy teenager who'd hog the
TV and pig out on Henry's biscuits?
Parents should just stay at home where
they belonged, thought Horrid Henry.

And now it looked like they would
have to. Ha! His parents were mean and
horrible, but he'd had a lot of practice
managing them. Babysitters were unpre-
dictable. Babysitters were hard work.
And by the time you'd broken them in
and shown them who was boss, for some
reason they didn't want to come any
more. The only good babysitters let you

stay up all night and eat sweets until you were sick. Sadly, Horrid Henry never got one of those.

"We have to find a babysitter," wailed Mum. "The party is tomorrow night. I've tried everyone. Who else is there?"

"There's got to be someone," said Dad. "Think!"

Mum thought.

Dad thought.

"What about Rebecca?" said Dad.

Horrid Henry's heart missed a beat. He stopped drawing moustaches on Perfect Peter's school pictures. Maybe

23

he'd heard wrong. Oh please, not
Rebecca! Not – Rabid Rebecca!

"Who did you say?" asked Henry. His
voice quavered.

"You heard me," said Dad. "Rebecca."

"NO!" screamed Henry. "She's horrible!"

"She's not horrible," said Dad. "She's
just – strict."

"There's no one else," said Mum grimly. "I'll phone Rebecca."

"She's a monster!" wailed Henry. "She
made Ralph go to bed at six o'clock!"

"I like going to bed at six o'clock," said
Perfect Peter. "After all, growing children
need their rest."

Horrid Henry growled and attacked.
He was the Creature from the Black

Lagoon, dragging the foolish mortal down to a watery grave.

"AAAEEEEE!" squealed Peter. "Henry pulled my hair."

"Stop being horrid, Henry!" said Dad. "Mum's on the phone."

Henry prayed. Maybe she'd be busy. Maybe she'd say no. Maybe she'd be dead. He'd heard all about Rebecca. She'd made Tough Toby get in his pyjamas at five o'clock *and* do all his homework. She'd unplugged Dizzy Dave's computer.

25

She'd made Moody Margaret wash the
floor. No doubt about it, Rabid Rebecca
was the toughest teen in town.

Henry lay on the rug and howled.
Mum shouted into the phone.

"You can! That's great, Rebecca. No,
that's just the TV – sorry for the noise.
See you tomorrow."

"NOOOOOOOOO!" wailed Henry.

Ding dong.

"I'll get it!" said Perfect Peter. He
skipped to the door.

Henry flung himself on the carpet.

"I DON'T WANT TO HAVE A
BABYSITTER!" he wailed.

The door opened. In walked the
biggest, meanest, ugliest, nastiest-looking
girl Henry had ever seen. Her arms were
enormous. Her head was enormous.
Her teeth were enormous. She looked
like she ate elephants for breakfasts,

27

crocodiles for lunch,
and snacked on
toddlers for tea.

"What have you
got to eat?" snarled
Rabid Rebecca.

Dad took a step back.
"Help yourself to anything in the fridge,"
said Dad.

"Don't worry, I will," said Rebecca.

"GO HOME, YOU WITCH!" howled
Henry.

"Bedtime is nine o'clock," shouted
Dad, trying to be heard above Henry's
screams. He edged his way carefully past
Rebecca, jumped over Henry, then
dashed out the front door.

"I DON'T WANT TO HAVE A
BABYSITTER!" shrieked Henry.

"Be good, Henry," said Mum weakly.
She stepped over Henry, then escaped
from the house.

The door closed.

Horrid Henry was alone in the house with Rabid Rebecca.

He glared at Rebecca.

Rebecca glared at him.

"I've heard all about you, you little creep," growled Rebecca. "No one bothers me when I'm babysitting."

Horrid Henry stopped screaming.

"Oh yeah," said Horrid Henry. "We'll see about that."

Rabid Rebecca bared her fangs. Henry recoiled. Perhaps I'd better keep out of her way, he thought, then slipped into the sitting room and turned on the telly.

Ahh, Mutant Max. Hurray! How bad could life be when a brilliant program like Mutant Max was on? He'd annoy Rebecca as soon as it was over.

Rebecca stomped into the room and snatched the clicker.

ZAP!

DA DOO, DA DOO DA, DA DOO DA DOO DA, tangoed some horrible spangly dancers.

"Hey," said Henry. "I'm watching Mutant Max."

"Tough," said Rebecca. "*I'm* watching ballroom dancing."

Snatch!

Horrid Henry grabbed the clicker.

ZAP!

"And it's mutants, mutants, mut — "

Snatch!

Zap!

DA DOO, DA DOO DA, DA DOO
DA DOO DA.

DOO, DA DOO DA, DA DOO DA
DOO DA.

Horrid Henry tangoed round the
room, gliding and sliding.

"Stop it," muttered Rebecca.

Henry shimmied back and forth in
front of the telly, blocking her view and
singing along as loudly as he could.

"DA DOO, DA DOO DA," warbled
Henry.

"I'm warning you," hissed Rebecca.

Perfect Peter walked in. He had
already put on his blue bunny pyjamas,
brushed his teeth and combed his hair.
He held a game of Chinese Checkers in
his hand.

"Rebecca, will you play a game with
me before I go to bed?" asked Peter.

"NO!" roared Rebecca. "I'm trying to
watch TV. Shut up and go away."

Perfect Peter leapt back.

"But I thought – since I was all ready for bed – " he stammered.

"I've got better things to do than to play with you," snarled Rebecca. "Now go to bed this minute, both of you."

"But it's not my bedtime for hours," protested Henry. "I want to watch Mutant Max."

"Nor mine," said Perfect Peter timidly. "There's this nature programme – "

"GO!" howled Rebecca.

"NO!" howled Henry.

"RAAAAA!" roared Rabid Rebecca.

Horrid Henry did not know how it happened. It was as if fiery dragon's breath had blasted him upstairs. Somehow, he was

in his pyjamas, in bed, and it was only
seven o'clock.

Rabid Rebecca switched off the light.
"Don't even think of moving from that
bed," she hissed. "If I see you, or hear
you, or even smell you, you'll be sorry
you were born. I'll stay
downstairs, you stay
upstairs, and that way
no one will get
hurt." Then she
marched out of the
room and slammed the
door.

Horrid Henry was so shocked he could
not move. He, Horrid Henry, the bull-
dozer of babysitters, the terror of teachers, the bully of brothers, was in bed,
lights out, at seven o'clock.

Seven o'clock! Two whole hours
before his bedtime! This was an outrage!
He could hear Moody Margaret shrieking

next door. He could hear Toddler Tom zooming about on his tricycle. No one went to bed at seven o'clock. Not even toddlers!

Worst of all, he was thirsty. So what if she told me to stay in bed, thought Horrid Henry. I'm thirsty. I'm going to go downstairs and get myself a glass of water. It's my house and I'll do what I want.

Horrid Henry did not move.

I'm dying of thirst here, thought Henry. Mum and Dad will come home and I'll

be a dried out old stick insect, and boy
will she be in trouble.

Horrid Henry still did not move.

Go on, feet, urged Henry, let's just step
on down and get a little ol' glass of water.
So what if that bogey babysitter said he
had to stay in bed.
What could she do to
him?

She could chop
off my head and
bounce it down
the stairs,
thought Henry.

Eeek.

Well, let her try.

Horrid Henry remembered who he
was. The boy who'd sent teachers shrieking from the classroom. The boy who'd
destroyed the Demon Dinner Lady. The
boy who had run away from home and
almost reached the Congo.

I will get up and get a drink of water, he thought.

Sneak. Sneak. Sneak.

Horrid Henry crept to the bedroom door.

Slowly he opened it a crack.

Creak.

Then slowly, slowly, he opened the door a bit more and slipped out.

ARGHHHHHH!

There was Rabid Rebecca sitting at the top of the stairs.

It's a trap, thought Henry. She was lying in wait for me. I'm dead, I'm finished, they'll find my bones in the morning.

Horrid Henry dashed back inside his room and awaited his doom.

Silence.

What was going on? Why hadn't Rebecca torn him apart limb from limb?

Horrid Henry opened his door a
fraction and peeped out.

Rabid Rebecca was still sitting huddled
at the top of the stairs. She did not
move. Her eyes were fixed straight ahead.

"Spi–spi–spider," she whispered. She
pointed at a big, hairy spider in front of
her with a trembling hand.

"It's huge," said Henry. "Really hairy
and horrible and wriggly and – "

"STOP!" squealed Rebecca. "Help me,
Henry," she begged.

Horrid Henry was not the fearless
leader of a pirate gang for nothing.

"If I risk my life and get rid of the
spider, can I watch Mutant Max?" said
Henry.

"Yes," said Rebecca.

"And stay up 'til my parents come home?"

"Yes," said Rebecca.

"And eat all the ice cream in the fridge?"

"YES!" shrieked Rebecca. "Just get rid of that – that – "

"Deal," said Horrid Henry.

He dashed to his room and grabbed a jar.

Rabid Rebecca hid her eyes as Horrid Henry scooped up the spider. What a beauty!

"It's gone," said Henry.

Rebecca opened her beady red eyes.

"Right, back to bed, you little brat!"

"What?" said Henry.

"Bed. Now!" screeched Rebecca.

"But we agreed..." said Henry.

"Tough," said Rebecca. "That was then."

"Traitor," said Henry.

He whipped out the spider jar from behind his back and unscrewed the lid.

"On guard!" he said.

"AAEEEE!" whimpered Rebecca.

Horrid Henry advanced menacingly towards her.

"NOOOOOOO!" wailed Rebecca, stepping back.

"Now get in that room and stay there," ordered Henry. "Or else."

Rabid Rebecca skedaddled into the bathroom and locked the door.

"If I see you or hear you or even smell you you'll be sorry you were born," said Henry.

"I already am," said Rabid Rebecca.

Horrid Henry spent a lovely evening in front of the telly. He watched scary movies. He ate ice cream and sweets and biscuits and crisps until he could stuff no more in.

Vroom vroom.

Oops. Parents home.

Horrid Henry dashed upstairs and leapt into bed just as the front door opened.

Mum and Dad looked around the sitting room, littered with sweet wrappers, biscuit crumbs and ice cream cartons.

"You did tell her to help herself," said Mum.

"Still," said Dad. "What a pig."

"Never mind," said Mum brightly, "at least she managed to get Henry to bed.

42

That's a first."

Rabid Rebecca staggered into the room.

"Did you get enough to eat?" said Dad.

"No," said Rabid Rebecca.

"Oh," said Dad.

"Was everything all right?" asked Mum.

Rebecca looked at her.

"Can I go now?" said Rebecca.

"Any chance you could babysit on

Saturday?" asked Dad hopefully.

"What do you think I am, crazy?" shrieked Rebecca.

SLAM!

Upstairs, Horrid Henry groaned.

Rats. It was so unfair. Just when he had a babysitter beautifully trained, for some reason they wouldn't come back.

3

HORRID HENRY'S RAID

"You're such a pig, Susan!"

"No I'm not! You're the pig!"

"You are!" squealed Moody Margaret.

"You are!" squealed Sour Susan.

"Oink!"

"Oink!"

All was not well at Moody Margaret's Secret Club.

Sour Susan and Moody Margaret glared at each other inside the Secret Club tent. Moody Margaret waved the empty biscuit tin in Susan's sour face.

"*Someone* ate all the biscuits," said Moody Margaret. "And it wasn't me."

"Well, it wasn't me," said Susan.

"Liar!"

"Liar!"

Margaret stuck out her tongue at Susan.

Susan stuck out her tongue at Margaret.

Margaret yanked Susan's hair.

"Oww! You horrible meanie!" shrieked Susan. "I hate you."

She yanked Margaret's hair.

"OWWW!" screeched Moody Margaret. "How dare you?"

They scowled at each other.

"Wait a minute," said Margaret. "You don't think – "

★

48

Not a million miles
away, sitting on a
throne inside the
Purple Hand fort
hidden behind
prickly branches,
Horrid Henry wiped a
few biscuit crumbs from his mouth and
burped. Um boy, nothing beat the taste
of an arch-enemy's biscuits.

The branches parted.

"Password!" hissed Horrid Henry.

"Smelly toads."

"Enter," said Henry.

The sentry entered and gave the secret
handshake.

"Henry, why – " began Perfect Peter.

"Call me by my title, Worm!"

"Sorry, Henry – I mean Lord High
Excellent Majesty of the Purple Hand."

"That's better," said Henry. He waved
his hand and pointed at the ground. "Be

seated, Worm."

"Why am I Worm and you're Lord High Excellent Majesty?"

"Because I'm the Leader," said Henry.

"I want a better title," said Peter.

"All right," said the Lord High Excellent Majesty, "you can be Lord Worm."

Peter considered.

"What about Lord High Worm?"

"OK," said Henry. Then he froze.

"Worm! Footsteps!"

Perfect Peter peeked through the leaves.

"Enemies approaching!" he warned.

Pounding feet paused outside the entrance.

"Password!" said Horrid Henry.

"Dog poo breath," said Margaret, bursting in. Sour Susan followed.

"That's not the password," said Henry.

"You can't come in," squeaked the sentry, a little late.

"You've been stealing the Secret Club biscuits," said Moody Margaret.

"Yeah, Henry," said Susan.

Horrid Henry stretched and yawned.

"Prove it."

Moody Margaret pointed to all the crumbs lying on the dirt floor.

"Where did all these crumbs come from, then?"

"Biscuits," said Henry.

"So you admit it!" shrieked Margaret.

"Purple Hand biscuits," said Henry. He pointed to the Purple Hand skull and crossbones biscuit tin.

"Liar, liar, pants on fire," said Margaret.

Horrid Henry fell to the floor and started rolling around.

"Ooh, ooh, my pants are on fire, I'm burning, call the fire brigade!" shouted Henry.

Perfect Peter dashed off.

"Mum!" he hollered. "Henry's pants are on fire!"

Margaret and Susan made a hasty retreat.

Horrid Henry stopped rolling and howled with laughter.

"Ha ha ha ha ha – the Purple Hand rules!" he cackled.

"We'll get you for this, Henry," said Margaret.

"Yeah, yeah," said Henry.

"You didn't really steal their biscuits, did you Henry?" asked Lord High Worm the following day.

"As if," said Horrid Henry. "Now get back to your guard duty. Our enemies may be planning a revenge attack."

"Why do I always have to be the guard?" said Peter. "It's not fair."

"Whose club is this?" said Henry fiercely.

Peter's lip began to tremble.

"Yours," muttered Peter.

"So if you want to stay as a temporary member, you have to do what I say," said Henry.

"OK," said Peter.

"And remember, one day, if you're very good, you'll be promoted from junior sentry to chief sentry," said Henry.

"Ooh," said Peter, brightening.

Business settled, Horrid Henry reached for the biscuit tin. He'd saved five yummy chocolate fudge chewies for today.

Henry picked up the tin and stopped. Why wasn't it rattling? He shook it.

Silence.

Horrid Henry ripped off the lid and shrieked.

The Purple Hand biscuit tin was empty. Except for one thing. A dagger drawn on a piece of paper. The dastardly

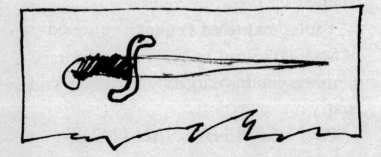

mark of Margaret's Secret Club! Well, he'd show them who ruled.

"Worm!" he shrieked. "Get in here!"

Peter entered.

"We've been raided!" screamed Henry. "You're fired!"

"Waaaah!" wailed Peter.

"Good work, Susan," said the Leader of the Secret Club, her face covered in chocolate.

"I don't see why you got three biscuits and I only got two when I was the one who sneaked in and stole them," said Susan sourly.

"Tribute to your Leader," said Moody Margaret.

"I still don't think it's fair," muttered Susan.

"Tough," said Margaret. "Now let's hear your spy report."

"NAH NAH NEE NAH NAH!"

screeched a voice from outside.

Susan and Margaret dashed out of the
Secret Club tent. They were too late.
There was Henry, prancing off, waving
the Secret Club banner he'd stolen.

"Give that back, Henry!" screamed
Margaret.

"Make me!" said Henry.

Susan chased him. Henry darted.

Margaret chased him. Henry dodged.

"Come and get me!" taunted Henry.

"All right," said Margaret. She walked

towards him, then suddenly jumped over
the wall into Henry's garden and ran to
the Purple Hand fort.

"Hey, get away from there!" shouted
Henry, chasing after her. Where was that
useless sentry when you needed him?

Margaret nabbed Henry's skull and
crossbones flag, and darted off.

The two Leaders faced each other.

"Gimme my flag!" ordered Henry.

"Gimme my flag!" ordered Margaret.

"You first," said Henry.

"*You* first," said Margaret.

Neither moved.

"OK, at the count of three we'll throw them to each other," said Margaret. One, two, three — throw!"

Margaret held on to Henry's flag.

Henry held on to Margaret's flag.

Several moments passed.

"Cheater," said Margaret.

"Cheater," said Henry.

"I don't know about you, but I have important spying work to get on with," said Margaret.

"So?" said Henry. "Get on with it. No one's stopping you."

"Drop my flag, Henry," said Margaret.

"No," said Henry.

"Fine," said Margaret. "Susan! Bring me the scissors."

Susan ran off.

"Peter!" shouted Henry. "Worm! Lord

Worm! Lord High Worm!"

Peter stuck his head out of the upstairs window.

"Peter! Fetch the scissors! Quick!" ordered Henry.

"No," said Peter. "You fired me, remember?" And he slammed the window shut.

"You're dead, Peter," shouted Henry.

Sour Susan came back with the scissors and gave them to Margaret. Margaret held the scissors to Henry's flag. Henry didn't budge. She wouldn't dare –

Snip!

Aaargh! Moody Margaret cut off a corner of Henry's flag. She held the scissors poised to make another cut.

Horrid Henry had spent hours painting his beautiful flag. He knew when he was beat.

"Stop!" shrieked Henry.

He dropped Margaret's flag. Margaret dropped his flag. Slowly, they inched towards each other, then dashed to grab their own flag.

"Truce?" said Moody Margaret, beaming.

"Truce," said Horrid Henry, scowling.

I'll get her for this, thought Horrid Henry. No one touches my flag and lives.

★

Horrid Henry watched and waited until it was dark and he heard the plinky-plonk sound of Moody Margaret practising her piano.

The coast was clear. Horrid Henry sneaked outside, jumped over the wall and darted inside the Secret Club Tent.

Swoop! He swept up the Secret Club pencils and secret code book.

Snatch! He snaffled the Secret Club stool.

Grab! He bagged the Secret Club biscuit tin.

Was that everything?

No!

Scoop! He snatched the Secret Club motto ("Down with boys").

Pounce! He pinched the Secret Club carpet.

Horrid Henry looked around. The Secret Club tent was bare.

Except for –

Henry considered. Should he?

Yes!

Whisk! The Secret Club tent collapsed. Henry gathered it into his arms with the rest of his spoils.

Huffing and puffing, gasping and panting, Horrid Henry staggered off over the wall, laden with the Secret Club.

Raiding was hot, heavy work, but a pirate had to do his duty. Wouldn't all this booty look great decorating his fort? A rug on the floor, an extra biscuit tin, a repainted motto – "Down with girls" – yes, the Purple Hand Fort would have to be renamed the Purple Hand Palace.

Speaking of which, where was the Purple Hand Fort?

Horrid Henry looked about wildly for the Fort entrance.

It was gone.

He searched for the Purple Hand throne.

It was gone.

And the Purple Hand biscuit tin – GONE!

There was a rustling sound in the shadows. Horrid Henry turned and saw a strange sight.

There was the Purple Hand Fort leaning against the shed.

What?!

Suddenly the Fort
started moving.
Slowly, jerkily, the
Fort wobbled
across the lawn
towards the wall
on its four new stumpy legs.

Horrid Henry was livid. How dare
someone try to nick his fort! This was an
outrage. What was the world coming to,
when people just sneaked into your garden and made off with your fort? Well,
no way!

Horrid Henry let out a pirate roar.

"RAAAAAAAA!" roared Horrid
Henry.

"AHHHHHHH!" shrieked the Fort.
CRASH!

The Purple Hand Fort fell to the
ground. The raiders ran off, squabbling.

"I told you to hurry, you lazy lump!"

"You're the lazy lump!"

Victory!

Horrid Henry climbed to the top of his fort and grabbed his banner. Waving it proudly, he chanted his victory chant:

NAH NAH NE NAH NAH!

4

HORRID HENRY'S CAR JOURNEY

"Henry! We're waiting!"

"Henry! Get down here!"

"Henry! I'm warning you!"

Horrid Henry sat on his bed and scowled. His mean, horrible parents could warn him all they liked. He wasn't moving.

"Henry! We're going to be late," yelled Mum.

"Good!" shouted Henry.

"Henry! This is your final warning," yelled Dad.

"I don't want to go to Polly's!" screamed Henry. "I want to go to Ralph's birthday party."

Mum stomped upstairs.

"Well you can't," said Mum. "You're coming to the christening, and that's that."

"NO!" screeched Henry. "I hate Polly, I hate babies, and I hate you!"

Henry had been a page boy at the wedding of his cousin, Prissy Polly, when she'd married Pimply Paul. Now they had a prissy, pimply baby, Vomiting Vera.

Henry had met Vera once before. She'd thrown up all over him. Henry had hoped never to see her again until she was grown up and behind bars, but no such luck. He had to go and watch her be dunked in a vat of water, on the

same day that Ralph was having a
birthday party at Goo-Shooter World.
Henry had been longing for ages to go
to Goo-Shooter World. Today was his
chance. His only chance. But no.
Everything was ruined.

Perfect Peter poked his head round the
door.

"*I'm* all ready, Mum," said Perfect Peter.
His shoes were polished, his teeth were
brushed, and his hair neatly combed.
"I know how annoying it is to be kept
waiting when you're in a rush."

"Thank you, darling Peter," said Mum.
"At least one of my children knows how
to behave."

Horrid Henry roared and attacked. He
was a swooping vulture digging his claws
into a dead mouse.

"AAAAAAAAAEEEEE!" squealed
Peter.

"Stop being horrid, Henry!" said Mum.

"No one told me it was today!" screeched Henry.

"Yes we did," said Mum. "But you weren't paying attention."

"As usual," said Dad.

"*I* knew we were going," said Peter.

"I DON'T WANT TO GO TO POLLY'S!" screamed Henry. "I want to go to Ralph's!"

"Get in the car – NOW!" said Dad.

"Or no TV for a year!" said Mum.

Eeek! Horrid Henry stopped wailing. No TV for a year. Anything was better than that.

Grimly, he stomped down the stairs and out the front door. They wanted him in the car. They'd have him in the car.

"Don't slam the door," said Mum.

SLAM!

Horrid Henry pushed Peter away from the car door and scrambled for the right-

hand side behind the driver. Perfect
Peter grabbed his legs and tried to climb
over him.

Victory! Henry got there first.

Henry liked sitting on the right-hand
side so he could watch the speedometer.

Peter liked sitting on the right-hand
side so he could watch the speedometer.

"Mum," said Peter. "It's my turn to sit
on the right!"

"No it isn't," said Henry. "It's mine."

71

"Mine!"

"Mine!"

"We haven't even left and already you're fighting?" said Dad.

"You'll take turns," said Mum. "You can swap after we stop."

Vroom. Vroom.

Dad started the car.

The doors locked.

Horrid Henry was trapped.

But wait. Was there a glimmer of hope? Was there a teeny tiny chance? What was it Mum always said when he and Peter were squabbling in the car? "If you don't stop fighting I'm going to turn around and go home!" And wasn't home just exactly where he wanted to be? All he had to do was to do what he did best.

"Could I have a story tape please?" said Perfect Peter.

"No! I want a music tape," said Horrid Henry.

"I want 'Mouse Goes to Town'," said Peter.

"I want 'Driller Cannibals' Greatest Hits'," said Henry.

"Story!"

"Music!"

"Story!"

"Music!"

SMACK!

SMACK!

"Waaaaaa!"

"Stop it, Henry," said Mum.

"Tell Peter to leave me alone!" screamed Henry.

"Tell Henry to leave *me* alone!" screamed Peter.

"Leave each other alone," said Mum.

Horrid Henry glared at Perfect Peter. Perfect Peter glared at Horrid Henry.

Horrid Henry stretched. Slowly, steadily, centimetre by centimetre, he spread out into Peter's area.

"Henry's on my side!"

"No I'm not!"

"Henry, leave Peter alone," said Dad. "I mean it."

"I'm not doing anything," said Henry. "Are we there yet?"

"No," said Dad.

Thirty seconds passed.

"Are we there yet?" said Horrid Henry.

"No!" said Mum.

"Are we there yet?" said Horrid Henry.

"NO!" screamed Mum and Dad.

"We only left ten minutes ago," said Dad.

Ten minutes! Horrid Henry felt as if they'd been travelling for hours.

"Are we a quarter of the way there yet?"

"NO!"

"Are we halfway there yet?"

"NO!!"

"How much longer until we're halfway there?"

"Stop it, Henry!" screamed Mum.

"You're driving me crazy!" screamed Dad. "Now be quiet and leave us alone."

Henry sighed. Boy, was this boring. Why didn't they have a decent car, with built-in video games, movies, and jacuzzi? That's just what he'd have, when he was king.

Softly, he started to hum under his breath.

"Henry's humming!"

"Stop being horrid, Henry!"

"I'm not doing anything," protested Henry. He lifted his foot.

"MUM!" squealed Peter. "Henry's kicking me."

"Are you kicking him, Henry?"

"Not yet," muttered Henry. Then he screamed.

"Mum! Peter's looking out of my window!"

"Dad! Henry's looking out of *my* window."

"Peter breathed on me."

"Henry's breathing loud on purpose."

"Henry's staring at me."

"Peter's on my side!"

"Tell him to stop!" screamed Henry and Peter.

Mum's face was red.

Dad's face was red.

"That's it!" screamed Dad.

"I can't take this anymore!" screamed Mum.

Yes! thought Henry. We're going to turn back!

But instead of turning round, the car screeched to a halt at the motorway services.

"We're going to take a break," said
Mum. She looked exhausted.

"Who needs a wee?" said Dad. He
looked even worse.

"Me," said Peter.

"Henry?"

"No," said Henry. He wasn't a baby.
He knew when he needed a wee and he
didn't need one now.

"This is our only stop, Henry," said
Mum. "I think you should go."

"NO!" screamed Henry. Several people

looked up. "I'll wait in the car."

Mum and Dad were too tired to argue. They disappeared into the services with Peter.

Rats. Despite his best efforts, it looked like Mum and Dad were going to carry on. Well, if he couldn't make them turn back, maybe he could *delay* them? Somehow? Suddenly Henry had a wonderful, spectacular idea. It couldn't be easier, and it was guaranteed to work. He'd miss the christening!

Mum, Dad, and Peter got back in the car. Mum drove off.

"I need a wee," said Henry.

"Not now, Henry."

"I NEED A WEE!" screamed Henry. "NOW!"

Mum headed back to the services.

Dad and Henry went to the toilets.

"I'll wait for you outside," said Dad. "Hurry up or we'll be late."

Late! What a lovely word.

Henry went into the toilet and locked the door. Then he waited. And waited. And waited.

Finally, he heard Dad's grumpy voice.

"Henry? Have you fallen in?"

Henry rattled the door.

"I'm locked in," said Henry. "The door's stuck. I can't get out."

"Try, Henry," pleaded Dad.

"I have," said Henry. "I guess they'll have to break the door down."

That should take a few hours. He

settled himself on the toilet seat and got
out a comic.

"Or you could just crawl underneath
the partition into the next stall," said
Dad.

Aaargghh. Henry could have burst into
tears. Wasn't it just his rotten luck to try
to get locked in a toilet which had gaps
on the sides? Henry didn't much fancy
wriggling round on the cold floor.
Sighing, he gave the stall door a tug and
opened it.

Horrid Henry sat in silence for the rest
of the trip. He was so depressed he didn't
even protest when Peter demanded his
turn on the right. Plus, he felt car sick.

Henry rolled down his window.

"Mum!" said Peter. "I'm cold."

Dad turned the heat on.

"Having the heat on makes me feel sick," said Henry.

"I'm going to be sick!" whimpered Peter.

"I'm going to be sick," whined Henry.

"But we're almost there," screeched Mum. "Can't you hold on until – "

Bleeeachh.

Peter threw up all over Mum.

Bleeeechhh. Henry threw up all over Dad.

The car pulled into the driveway. Mum and Dad staggered out of the

car to Polly's front
door.

"We survived,"
said Mum, mopping
her dress.

"Thank God that's
over," said Dad, mopping
his shirt.

Horrid Henry scuffed his feet sadly
behind them. Despite all his hard work,
he'd lost the battle. While Rude Ralph
and Dizzy Dave and Jolly Josh were dash-
ing about spraying each other with green
goo later this afternoon he'd be stuck at a
boring party with lots of grown-ups yak
yak yaking. Oh misery!

Ding dong.

The door opened.
It was Prissy Polly.
She was in her
bathrobe and slippers.
She carried a stinky,

83

smelly, wailing baby over her shoulder. Pimply Paul followed. He was wearing a filthy T-shirt with sick down the front.

"Eeeek," squeaked Polly.

Mum tried to look as if she had not been through hell and barely lived to tell the tale.

"We're here!" said Mum brightly. "How's the lovely baby?"

"Too prissy," said Polly.

"Too pimply," said Paul.

Polly and Paul looked at Mum and Dad.

"What are you doing here?" said Polly finally.

"We're here for the christening," said Mum.

"Vera's christening?" said Polly.

"It's *next* weekend," said Paul.

Mum looked like she wanted to sag to the floor.

Dad looked like he wanted to sag beside her.

"We've come on the wrong day?" whispered Mum.

"You mean, we have to go and come back?" whispered Dad.

"Yes," said Polly.

"Oh no," said Mum.

"Oh no," said Dad.

"Bleeeach," vomited Vera.

"Eeeek!" wailed Polly. "Gotta go." She slammed the door.

"You mean, we can go home?" said Henry. "Now?"

"Yes," whispered Mum.

"Whoopee!" screamed Henry. "Hang on, Ralph, here I come!"

The HORRID HENRY books
by Francesca Simon

Illustrated by Tony Ross
Each book contains four stories

HORRID HENRY

Henry is dragged to dancing class against his will; vies with Moody Margaret to make the yuckiest Glop, goes camping in France and tries to be good like Perfect Peter — but not for long.

HORRID HENRY AND THE SECRET CLUB

Horrid Henry gets an injection, torments his little brother Perfect Peter, creates havoc at his own birthday party, and plans sweet revenge when Moody Margaret won't let him into her Secret Club.

HORRID HENRY'S NITS

Scratch. Scratch. Scratch. Horrid Henry has nits – and he's on a mission to give them to everyone else too. After that, he can turn his attention to wrecking the school trip, ruining his parents' dinner party, and terrifying Perfect Peter.

HORRID HENRY GETS RICH QUICK

(Originally published as *Horrid Henry Strikes It Rich*) Horrid Henry tries to sell off Perfect Peter and get rich, makes sure he gets the presents he wants for Christmas, sabotages Sports Day at school – and runs away from home.